PUMPKIN SPICE MURDER

The Frosted Love Cozy Mystery Series, Book 17

SUMMER PRESCOTT

D1636818

Summer Prescott Books Publishing

6o-something Resident Artist, Phillip Kellerman, entered *Cupcakes in Paradise* with nothing on his mind beyond scoring a couple of cupcakes. He'd seen on the sign in the window that the Cupcake of the Day was a Pumpkin Spice with Cream Cheese filling, and his mouth watered in anticipation. Couple that with a cup of Missy Gladstone-Beckett's fresh brewed Costa Rican coffee, and he was ready to settle in for an hour or so, chatting up the lovely blonde proprietor and catching her up on any juicy bits of gossip that might be happening in the sleepy town of Calgon, Florida.

"What manner of flame-haired goddess is this?" his

voice boomed, filling the cozy eating area of the tea room, upon seeing Echo, Missy's best friend, manning the counter. He hurried to the counter, introduced himself to a bemused Echo and made a grand gesture of kissing her hand.

"Hello," she chuckled, eyebrows raised at the flamboyant stranger. "Can I help you with something?" she asked, not sure she wanted to hear his answer.

"My dear, the mere presence of such a beautiful creature has helped me more than you could know," Kel grinned, staring at her with unabashed admiration.

"Morning, Kel," Missy breezed in from the kitchen, having heard his voice and wanting to introduce him to her best friend. "I see you've met Echo. She's visiting from California and helping me out while she's here," she explained, trying not to giggle at his awestruck expression.

"Echo," he mused nodding. "Indeed, I think that lovely face will *echo* in my thoughts forever more," he announced, while the subject of his admiration squirmed a bit under the lavish torrent of compliments.

"So...cupcakes?" she asked, trying to guide the oddly charming artist back to safer territory.

"Cupcakes indeed, My Goddess," he nodded gravely. "Two Pumpkin Spice, and please be kind enough to reassure me that there is freshly brewed Costa Rican about," he blinked at her, apparently still spellbound.

"Of course there is," Missy came to the rescue. "Would I ever disappoint you by not having a fresh pot ready at precisely 9:05?" she asked.

"You are too kind, madam," he gave her a slight bow and accepted the plate of cupcakes from Echo.

"I try, Kel," she smiled and poured a steaming mug of coffee for the dapper gent, who had ensconced himself at a table with a direct view of Echo behind the counter. He opened his newspaper and pretended to absorb himself in the news, but Missy knew better. Mornings were for cupcakes, coffee, and gossip in Kel's world. She couldn't wait to sit down for the daily update, but felt as though she owed Echo an explanation.

"Echo, could you come help me in the back for a second?" she asked, heading for the kitchen.

"Of course," her friend murmured, trailing behind and glancing back over her shoulder at the character in the tea room, who waved when he caught her gaze. Blushing a deep pink, she hurried after her friend.

"Okay, so what's with that guy?" Echo asked, intrigued, despite herself.

"He's a local artist – very talented, and a bit eccentric, but positively harmless," Missy reassured her still-flushed friend.

"He's kind of handsome, in a distinguished and slightly theatrical way," Echo mused, shrugging.

"Sweetie, he's in his early 60's..." her friend pointed out.

"Well, maybe there's something to be said for age and experience," she countered, eyebrows raised.

"Oh, my...it's been a long time, hasn't it honey?" Missy challenged, trying to bring her friend back to reality.

"Longer than you can imagine," was the wry reply.

"Well, it's morning gossip time, you're welcome to participate if you'd like," Missy offered, heading back to the front.

"Morning gossip time? That doesn't sound like something you'd typically approve of," Echo noted.

"It's harmless. He just comes in and tells me all about who's getting married, who got dumped, who died and who's moving in or out of town. I'm learning a lot about the local community actually," she grinned mischievously.

"I'm in," the lonely redhead nodded with a sly smile.

"Okay, Kel, spill it...what's going on in our scandalous little town today?" Missy asked, sitting down with her cup of coffee. Echo sat across from her and looked at the gent expectantly.

"It's a wonderful day when I'm treated to the gracious company of two beautiful ladies," he commented, folding his paper and take a sip of coffee. "It seems that our new police chief has purchased the old Fenton house for his lovely wife and four children. Last I'd heard it was still tied up in probate, but mysteriously all that muck cleared up just in time for the incoming chief to purchase it," he rolled his eyes dramatically.

"Well, that's good. Chas says he seems to be a good guy," Missy nodded.

"Which will be a bit of a refreshing change after the last chief," Kel replied cattily. "There have also been rumors of an imminent divorce," he announced gravely.

"Awww...that's too bad," Missy said, plucking a bite from her cupcake. "Who?"

"Blanche and Frederick Palmer," he confided, shaking his head. "And I daresay that the former Mrs. Palmer would disagree with your assessment of it being a bad thing. She's been more than ready to call it quits for years. The only reason that it's lasted as long as it has is because she travels so much that they rarely see each other. Far be it from me to spread rumors...but it's going around in the social circles that dear Fred has his eye set on our mutual friend, Carla Mayhew," he announced with a disapproving air.

Missy's mouth fell open for a moment. "Carla? Oh my, as if that woman hasn't had enough to deal with recently," she sighed.

Echo swallowed a bite of cupcake and muttered sarcastically, "Oh, poor dear. Karma's a..."

Her friend interrupted before she could finish the unkind thought. "Echo and Carla met a couple of weeks ago and didn't exactly feel an instant warmth," she explained, as Kel gazed at Echo speculatively.

A slow grin broke across Kel's face. "Is that so?" he asked, seemingly amused at the thought. "Oil and water, eh? I can see how that might happen," he chuckled. "Well, lovely ladies," he said, putting his coffee cup on top of his empty cupcake plate. "Alas, duty calls. I'm preparing for a showing this weekend," he dug in his pocket and produced a small postcard, handing it to Missy. "Here's the location – I'd be more than honored by your presence, should you choose to attend," he bowed, kissing first Missy's hand, then Echo's, lingering just a bit. "Until the morrow," he inclined his head, then turned and strolled out the door.

"What a character," Missy remarked when the door shut behind his retreating form.

"Yes, he is," Echo nodded with blatant interest.

"Oh, boy...." Missy sighed.

Chapter 2

*S*omehow, Carla Mayhew seemed to know that Echo left *Cupcakes in Paradise* early on Tuesday afternoons, so she'd pop in to visit with Missy. The two had met when Carla, a tiny, energetic brunette, who was an Interior Decorator, had redone some of the rooms in the bed and breakfast inn that Missy and her husband, the handsome and clever Detective Chas Beckett owned, as well as the owner's wing of the inn. The poor woman's husband and son had been murdered all-too-recently, but she seemed to be coping better and better as time progressed.

"Hey, girl," Missy greeted Carla with a hug when she came in. "I saved a Lemon Raspberry cupcake for you," she said, heading behind the counter.

"Oh, my, that sounds amazing. I'm in desperate need of some carb therapy right now," the weary decorator sighed.

"Yikes, rough day at the office?" Missy asked, setting down a plated cupcake and a delicate china cup and saucer of Earl Grey tea.

"Definitely. I was working with Marge Belkens today on her parlor. The poor woman is color blind and without even calling to ask me about it, she purchased an Italian silk couch online a couple of weeks ago. It came in today, and doesn't coordinate with anything else in the room. It cost her ten thousand dollars and she insists that we make it work. Her husband came in to check on the progress of the room and flipped out when he saw the mismatched couch, blaming me for not coming up with a cohesive design. I could just tear my hair out," Carla exclaimed, pulling her cupcake into two pieces.

"Well, don't do that, sugar, just keep taking it out on that cupcake," Missy grinned. "Sounds like you need a drink, not a cupcake," she teased.

"Don't tempt me," the decorator shot back dryly. "What's new in your world? Please tell me something sweet and heartwarming to restore my faith in humanity, I beg you."

"Well, Kel met Echo yesterday...that was an interesting experience," Missy giggled.

"Oh, my...there's a match made in Hades," Carla made a face.

Missy looked at her for a long moment. It wasn't like her to be so negative. "Are you okay, sweetie?" she asked, concerned. "You seem really down."

"I'll be fine," Carla replied, dropping her head into

her hand. "I'm just tired of all of the stupid drama that my clients cause over trivial things. I'm so tempted sometimes to just snap and remind them that some of us have actual trauma in our lives and still try to be pleasant and do the right thing," she grumbled, rubbing her temples.

"That's understandable," Missy nodded. "You've been through more in the past several weeks than most people deal with in an entire lifetime," she said sympathetically. "Maybe you should take some time off...go on vacation," she suggested.

"You're probably right, but I have a couple of projects that I need to complete before I can even think about it," she replied, staring into her cup of tea.

"What are you doing tonight? Would you like to come over for dinner? I think Chas is planning on grilling some steaks – you should join us," Missy offered, thinking that a night among friends might be just the thing to help lift her spirits.

"You're grilling steaks with a vegan in the house?" Carla said coolly, raising an eyebrow.

"Well, there'll be a veggie burger for Echo," she explained, wondering what had spurred the instant animosity between her two girlfriends.

The decorator rolled her eyes but let it go. "Thanks, but I'll have to pass. I'm going to try to make some progress on some of my designs tonight," she made an excuse that was patently obvious in its insincerity, but Missy didn't press her further.

"Okay, well...if you change your mind, just give me a call and we'll throw an extra steak on the fire for you," she smiled, feeling oddly sad.

"Thanks, Missy. You're one of the few bright spots in

my life right now, and I appreciate you more than you know," her usually reserved friend commented.

Carla's simple admission touched Missy's heart, and she reached across the table to cover her friend's hand with hers. It was a lovely moment that was shattered by the chime over the door, followed by a storm of a human being barging in.

"Where is he?" an artificially blonde, clearly wealthy woman demanded of Carla, startling both her and Missy.

"Where's who?" a befuddled Missy asked.

"He said he was going out to lunch, and then you disappeared right after he did, you little tart," the woman seethed, ignoring Missy altogether. "You had better tell me right now where the lying little snake is," she ordered, teeth clenched.

Missy looked from the furious blonde's face to Carla's impassive one.

"I have no idea what you're talking about, Blanche. As you can see, I'm here and Freddie is not. What more do you want?" Carla challenged mildly.

"Freddie? Freddie? Well, isn't that just adorable? I'm his wife and I don't even call him that," Blanche Palmer hissed with accusation.

Carla sighed. "You know that we've known each other since high school. Look in his yearbook sometime...everyone called him that," she informed the ruffled hen calmly.

Blanche thrust a well-manicured finger with hot-pink nail polish gracing the tip into Carla's face. To her credit, the decorator didn't even flinch. "You listen to me, you moneygrubbing little wretch...he only wants one thing from you, and it's not a new paint color for the den. Make no mistake, you don't have a chance for something meaningful with someone like Frederick. In case you hadn't noticed, he sets his sights way higher than the likes of you," she sniffed rudely. "And if I find out that you've tried to snare him with your...wiles, it will not go well for you. Or him," she warned, her eyes turning into slits of sheer hatred.

"So....color consultation tomorrow then?" Carla asked, rising to the full height of her 5'2" stature, which still left her looking up to the tall, thin blonde, hands on hips.

"Yeah, try showing your face in my home, sweetheart, see what happens," Blanche threatened, before turning on her heel and stalking from the shop.

Missy and Carla stared, unspeaking, as the socialite flung herself into her very expensive German sports car and screeched away from the curb. Missy turned slowly and looked at her friend.

"You okay?" she asked.

Carla burst into tears and threw herself into Missy's arms.

Chapter 3

*C*arla Mayhew walked slowly up the stairs in the darkened home, trailing her fingers along the banister with some trepidation. She'd been excited to be awarded the job of re-decorating the old Fenton house for the new police chief and his wife, and hoped that she hadn't been chosen out of pity, but now that she was here in the house, alone, she couldn't shake the chill that gripped her. She didn't believe in ghosts, so the rumors of the house being haunted hadn't bothered her a bit when she sent in her bid for re-doing the interior, but even she had to admit that there seemed to be a pall within the grey and faded walls.

The decorator's mission for today was to take photos

and measurements so that she could come up with a comprehensive plan for the renovation. The house was massive, set far back from the road, down a graveled drive, shrouded by trees dripping with moss. It was Victorian in style, but the new owners were looking for creative ways to update, while still paying homage to the period of the home. It was a challenging project, with many rooms to consider, but Carla loved a challenge, and historic homes were a particular favorite.

The wind moaned outside, heralding the onset of Fall, and the decorator shivered as the house seemed to creak and moan with it. The electricity had been turned on in the dreary place, but the old-fashioned lighting was inadequate, turning every surface greyer than it actually was. Hearing a squeak of floorboards above, Carla paused, heart thumping in her chest.

"Hello?" she said, well aware of how timid and fragile her voice sounded in the cavernous space. Of course, there was no answer. Telling herself that it was merely the sound of an old house settling, she continued up the stairs, unconsciously straining to listen for other mysterious noises. Finally, reaching the upstairs hall which overlooked the main foyer without further incident, she consulted her floor plan and turned left, headed toward the Master bedroom, where she intended to start.

The room was huge, like the rest of the house, but dark and cold, with intricately designed black wallpaper and heavy wood furnishings. It smelled musty, and Carla made a note that the duct work would have to be inspected, and new windows were a must. She made her way to the inadequate little Master bath, which featured a peeling and chipping claw foot tub with rust stains covering the bottom, and an ancient sink and toilet. Curious, she turned the calcium encrusted cold water spigot on the bathroom sink, only to have a grey sludge gurgle out of the faucet. The pipes banged suddenly with the effort, making her jump, and behind her in the bedroom, the door slammed.

Carla glanced up into the crackled antique mirror above the malfunctioning sink and saw how round and terrified her eyes were. Her heart beat so fast that she thought she might faint, and she took several deep breaths in the interest of self-preservation.

"Who's there?" she called, summoning every ounce of courage within her. Silence. She eyed the bathroom door, wondering what horror awaited her on the other side of it, and practically held her breath, listening. Placing her hand on the door knob, she slowly turned, wincing at the shotgun-loud squawk that the battered piece of brass made, shattering the silence. A cold feeling settled in her gut as she imagined the possible outcomes of her actions, but she gingerly swung the door open, and saw...nothing. No one was in the bedroom, there were no footprints in the dust other than hers, and, though the door was closed, when she'd left it open, nothing seemed to be out of place. She let out a sigh of relief, convinced now that the incident had to have been caused by nothing more than a particularly strong draft. Leaving it closed, she quickly took photos of the interior, along with measurements of the bedroom and bath and headed out, ready to move on to the next room.

When she placed her hand on the door knob, she was struck by how cold it felt to the touch. She tried to turn it to the left to open the door, but it wouldn't move, then she tried to turn it to the right, with the same result. Trying not to panic, she wiggled it back and forth with both hands, desperately trying to open the door. A startled spider dropped down from the top of the door casing, landing on her cheek and she screamed, brushing it away, dropping her bag and camera, waving her hands madly.

The door thrust open suddenly and Carla screamed again, seriously spooking the housekeeper who stood on the other side.

"Oh, my gosh!" the twenty-something young girl in jeans and a pink "Marvelous Maid Service" t-shirt shrieked, holding a hand up defensively and cringing.

Carla nearly collapsed with relief upon seeing an

innocent young woman on the other side of the door, rather than a serial killer or a demon straight from the pits of Hell.

"I'm so sorry," she panted, trying to catch her breath while she knelt on the filthy floor, stuffing her tape measure, camera and paint samples back in her bag.

"You must be the decorator," the woman grinned, recovering. "They told me that you would be here – I just didn't see you when I came in," she explained. "I'm Jessica, the housekeeper," she held out her hand to help Carla to her feet.

"Nice to meet you," she said, looking all over the place for the wayward spider, shuddering. "So, it must've been you who closed the door a few minutes ago," she remarked.

"This door? No, I was working in the nursery. I heard

this one slam and figured it was either a ghost or the wind, but I didn't touch it," she said earnestly.

Carla stared at her, having heard her words, but rejecting the implication that they carried. She knew that ghosts didn't exist, there had to be some other explanation. "Are you going to be okay here alone?" she asked Jessica, feeling really bad about leaving the young woman, but refusing to stay another minute.

"Sure, I'll be fine," the housekeeper assured the nervous decorator. "I've worked in lots of old houses like this. Generally, if you're respectful of them, they're respectful of you," she shrugged.

Not knowing what Jessica meant, and truthfully, not wanting to know, Carla pasted on a strained smile and trotted down the stairs as fast as she could go, vowing to design the rooms from the blue prints.

Chapter 4

"I love autumn," Echo sighed as she and Missy painted monster faces on pumpkins to decorate *Cupcakes in Paradise.*

"Me too," her friend agreed wholeheartedly. "For some reason, it makes me feel nostalgic. It's going to be strange though, being in a place where I don't see huge trees with leaves of gold and orange and red," Missy mused.

This would be her very first Fall since she moved from Louisiana to Florida, and while she loved the beautiful sunshine and blue skies, there was something a bit strange about planning for Halloween while wearing short sleeves and sandals.

"We really should start thinking about costumes for the masquerade, you know," she reminded her free-spirited friend.

"Are you sure that it'll be okay for me to attend? I mean, I've never met the chief of police, and the invitation was addressed to you and Chas..." she said, not wanting to intrude.

"Of course it's okay," Missy assured her. "Chas talked to him about it, and he and his wife are both dying to meet you," she said, putting down her paint brush and wiping her hands on a kitchen towel. "I just can't figure out what Chas and I should wear," she made a face.

"A costume, silly," Echo chuckled, excited at the idea of being able to dress up.

"Well, thanks, that was helpful," Missy tossed the towel at her. "I'm going to run to the back for cupcakes. Vegan mango?" she asked.

"Perfect," was the enthusiastic reply.

No sooner had Missy disappeared into the kitchen than the door chimes rang out, heralding the arrival of Chas Beckett.

"Hey, stranger," Echo greeted him warmly. "The boss lady is in the back getting some sustenance for her poor overworked helper," she joked.

"That's how she rolls," he replied with a smile, seeming distracted and making a beeline for the kitchen.

"Hey, beautiful," he surprised his wife with a kiss on the back of her neck as she reached for Echo's cupcake.

"Mmmm...hello yourself," she grinned. "I'm getting cupcakes, better claim one now if you're hungry," she waggled a Cinnamon Custard cupcake in front of his nose to tempt him.

"I'd love to, but I'm in a hurry," he replied apologetically. "Have you heard from Carla today?"

"No, I haven't heard from Carla in a while, why?" Catching his somber mood, she felt a cold chill run through her that had nothing to do with the autumn breeze outside her window.

"There was an accident over at the Fenton house – I don't have time to explain right now, but if you hear from her, will you have her call me, please? It's important," he said, kissing her lightly and turning to head out.

"Of course," Missy nodded. "Is everything okay?" she worried.

"We'll have to wait and see," he sighed.

"Bye, Chas," Echo called out as he sped by on his way to the door.

"Take care, Echo," he responded, his walk turning to a trot once he got outside.

"What was that all about?" she asked when Missy sat back down with their cupcakes.

"I have no idea."

Chapter 5

*P*hillip Kellerman was clearly enjoying being master of his own domain. His art show was a runaway success, and he'd sold nearly all of his work on the first day, taking so many commissions for future projects that he'd be busy for months. Reveling in his success was something in which he took great pleasure, and he worked the crowd at the exclusive gallery like a pro. The gallery staff made sure that hors d'oeuvres were fresh and plentiful, glasses were filled, and the exhibits were not touched, photographed, or otherwise disturbed. The show had received international acclaim and Kel was riding high, schmoozing potential buyers from Michigan to Morocco with his trademark grace and flair.

He saw a flash of silken copper in the midst of the crowd and excused himself from a conversation that was potentially worth tens of thousands of dollars. While Kel loved success, his priorities didn't center upon money. His preference was to make just enough to enjoy his life without undue worry, and talking to the stunning woman who just walked in had suddenly taken top priority to any sort of business deal that might have been proposed.

"Echo, Missy, you're both positively radiant this evening," he purred, trading his typical kiss on the hand for a warm embrace.

"Thanks, Kel," Missy smiled. "It certainly looks like you have a great turnout tonight," she observed, plucking two flutes of champagne from a tray and handing one to Echo.

"Indeed," he nodded, pleased. "The whole shebang seems to have evolved quite well," he agreed, taking a flute of champagne for himself. "Shall we toast?" he asked.

"Of course," Missy and Echo responded in unison, exchanged a look and giggled.

"To the most beautiful women in the room," he raised his glass, catching and holding Echo's gaze for a long moment. Then he leaned in and whispered theatrically. "But don't let the old bird in the lavender dress know that I said that...she has quite the fat checkbook," he winked mischievously, then moved on to greet more arrivals.

"He's hilarious," Missy remarked, watching him go.

"And talented," Echo breathed, looking around at the various pieces that surrounded the cocktail area.

Chas came in the door just then, and Missy waved to get his attention.

"Sorry I'm late," he kissed her warmly. "Duty never calls at a convenient time," he grumbled good-naturedly.

"I understand," Missy gazed at her husband fondly. "I'm just glad that you could make it," she assured him, handing him her champagne. "Here, you take this, I'll go snag another."

"That's not necessary. I'd be more than happy to get you…" the detective tried to protest, but was shut down when his doting wife raised her hand to silence him.

"I know you'd be more than happy to get me a drink, but I got here first, which means you have some catching up to do, so drink up, Buttercup, and I'll be right back," she ordered playfully.

Chuckling, the handsome husband did as he was told, enjoying the bubbles tickling his tastebuds.

Missy had to search for a few minutes to find a waiter with filled glasses of bubbly on his tray, and by the time she wended her way back to Chas, she found him in conversation with Carla, and found it strange that she had her hand on his arm in a familiar way.

"Carla, I didn't realize you were coming to the showing tonight," she remarked happily, glad that her friend had broken contact with her husband when she approached.

The decorator smiled, and seemed to have had quite her share of champagne already. She leaned in close and stage-whispered to Missy. "I had to come support Kel – he's been producing some major pieces for my clients. He may be as weird as they come, but he makes me look really good," she pursed her lips and nodded sagely.

"Well, I'm sure he'll be glad to see you here," Missy replied, subtly leaning away from the fumes emanating from Carla.

"Nah, I think he thinks that I'm an opinionated pain in the petunias, but we make each other money, so he puts up with me," she slurred.

"Are you okay?" she asked, feeling as though the decorator was a ticking time bomb just waiting to go off and do something socially inappropriate. With the rumors already circulating about her, she really couldn't afford to be the object of unkind scrutiny.

"I'm fine," she breathed, bathing Missy in an alcohol haze. "I'm just gonna go say hi to King Kel, and be on my way," she waved a hand in the air.

"You didn't drive, did you?" she worried.

"What are you tryin' to say?" the inebriated decorator challenged, eyebrow raised. She staggered slightly, then caught herself.

"I'm not implying anything," Missy assured her. "I just want to make sure that you get home safely."

"Well, then, lucky fer you, Mr. Jazzy Chazzy over there is gonna take me home," she gave a lopsided grin, patting the front of Chas's sport coat.

Missy gave Chas a curious glance and he nodded imperceptibly.

"Well, good. I won't keep you then," she said coolly, moving to her husband's side and twining her arm through his. Carla smirked, and moved slowly and carefully through the crowd, seeking out Kel.

"She asked for a ride, and I couldn't say no, given the condition that she's in," Chas explained with a grimace.

"I understand," Missy nodded. "I can go with you when you take her and then we can just head home from her house."

"What about Echo?"

"We'll take Carla home in your car, and Echo can bring my car back when she's done socializing."

"Sounds like a plan," the detective nodded. "Where is Echo, anyway?" he asked, scanning the room.

"Last I saw, she was looking at the exhibit," Missy replied.

Just then a commotion began, and a large sculpture swayed, tilted precariously, and crashed to the floor.

In the melee, she caught a brief glimpse of flame-colored hair firmly in the grasp of one drunken Carla Mayhew.

Chapter 6

"This piece is breathtaking," Echo marveled to Kel, who had attached himself, like Velcro, to her elbow from the moment she'd arrived.

"Somehow, I knew that you'd like this one," he gave her a mysterious smile.

"Really? Why?" she asked, taking a small sip of champagne.

"Look at the title, dear sprite," he said.

"California," she nodded. "I totally see it – the color – the quality of light spiraling through it – the vibrance and energy...you nailed it," she beamed, unexpected tears springing to her eyes.

"Oh, dear," Kel exclaimed, seeing the moisture welling. "Have I made you homesick?" he asked, concerned.

Echo laughed and wiped her eyes. "No, not at all. You've made me realize that wherever I am, everything about California that I love stays with me. It's beautiful," she said softly, biting her lower lip.

Kel was about to speak when a raucous voice shattered the moment. "What stays with you?" Carla scoffed. "Bean farts and tofu?" she snickered as Echo and Kel turned to her, stunned.

"Hmm...seems as though our little decorator needs to go sleep it off," the artist remarked, eyebrow raised in disapproval.

"Oh, don't be so darn stuffy," Carla slurred.

"I could walk you out and call a cab for you," Echo offered, trying to help.

"I can't think of a situation where I would ever want that to happen," the decorator replied nastily.

"Seriously, let me help," the gracious redhead insisted, reaching for Carla's arm.

Flinging her arm out of Echo's reach, Carla shoved the shocked woman hard, screaming, "Don't tell me what to do!"

Echo's arms flailed for a moment as she tried to catch her balance, but she stumbled back, bumping into "California" and careened toward the floor as the sculpture, swayed, tilted and came crashing down. Carla grabbed a handful of Echo's hair as she fell, and tumbled down on top of her as she slammed to the ground on top of the sculpture.

Echo tried to sit up, pushing hard against the limp weight of a very drunk interior decorator, and started to panic when she found herself wedged between Carla and California, unable to move. Chas appeared almost instantly and lifted the decorator off of a dazed Echo. The drunk woman flung her arms around his broad shoulders, burrowed her face into his neck and slurred, "My hero." Kel, thoroughly disgusted with Carla, and clearly concerned about Echo, knelt beside the humiliated redhead, whose cheeks, at the moment, competed with the fire of her hair.

"Good gracious, my dear, are you okay?" he asked, peering down at the fallen woman, whose high color served only to make her more beautiful.

"Well, my pride certainly smarts a bit," she sighed, taking the artist's hand and letting him help her to her feet. She was quite sore from having fallen on the metal and acrylic sculpture, and winced, placing her hand on her lower back.

"Do you need a hospital? I'll take you myself," Kel fussed over her.

Echo shook her head. "No. I think a warm bath will do the trick. There's a hot tub at the inn– I'm sure Missy won't mind if I soak in it for a bit," she assured the worried artist.

"Of course you can," Missy nodded, hugging her gently, all the while keeping an eye on Carla as she hung limply against Chas. "We need to get her home before something worse happens to her," she muttered, frowning. "Will you be able to drive?"

Before Echo could answer, Kel stepped in. "I will make certain that she returns safely to the inn," he decreed in a tone that brooked no nonsense.

"Thanks, Kel. You're the best," Missy exclaimed, kissing him on the cheek. "Echo, honey, you be careful. As soon as we get this...mess home, I'll come down to the hot tub and join you. I could use a little relaxation myself," she grimaced.

"Sounds good," her friend nodded, massaging her lower back. "Oh, hey, Missy!"

"What is it?"

"You might want to bring along a bucket, Betty Boozer over there is looking a little green," Echo pointed out, noting that Chas was keeping her on her feet while trying to keep his distance.

"Good call," Missy agreed, shaking her head at the spectacle.

Chapter 7

*C*has had stopped his car three times on the way to Carla's house so that the decorator could stumble to the side of the road and heave. Missy sat staring straight ahead each time, her compassion having deserted her when she saw the way that the drunk woman had treated her friend and her husband. They finally made it to her house and helped her inside, taking off her shoes and placing her gently on the couch, bucket at her side. She passed out the moment her head hit the upholstery, and Missy and Chas left her snoring softly.

Missy was more than a bit surprised when she arrived at the pool area and found that Echo wasn't alone. Apparently, Kel had brought his swim trunks along and was keeping the bruised and abraded woman company.

"Hey, you two," she greeted them, easing down into the hot, bubbling water. "Oh, my, this is just what the doctor ordered," she breathed, easing her head back as the water burbled over her shoulders.

"I'm feeling better already," Echo agreed.

"I can't believe Carla's behavior tonight," Missy shook her head. "I mean, I know that she just lost her husband and son, but I'm really shocked that she overindulged and made an utter fool of herself."

"And of me," her friend replied glumly, blushing at the memory of the incident.

"Nonsense," Kel responded firmly before Missy had the chance. "There wasn't a soul present who blamed you for that debacle. If anything, they most likely applauded the grace with which you handled the awkward situation," he assured her.

"Absolutely," Missy backed him up.

"I'm just so upset that your sculpture was ruined though," Echo told Kel.

"Well, you inspired it, and you've inspired the revision as well," he smiled at her from the opposite side of the tub.

"The revision?" Missy asked, taking a sip from the bottle of water that she'd brought along.

"Indeed. Just like the lovely woman who inspired it initially, "California" shall rise from the ashes of destruction like a glorious phoenix," he proclaimed with a twinkle in his eye.

"So, you're remaking it? That's amazing – I love that idea," she enthused as Echo blushed.

"Some things are worth the effort," Kel replied, glancing over at the very pink redhead.

Seeing her friend's obvious discomfort, Missy decided to save the day by changing the subject. "So, are you going to the new police chief's Halloween masquerade?" she asked the smitten artist.

"Naturally. I wouldn't miss it. Despite her poor choices this evening, I can't wait to see what Carla has done with the old Fenton place, she's been very hush-hush about it," he groused.

"Apparently, the party is sort of an excuse for the grand reveal," Missy said. "I'm really curious about it too. Carla said that when she went inside for the first time, she could see why people have said that it's haunted."

"Didn't someone get seriously injured in that house while she was there?" Kel asked, looking for a tidbit of gossip.

Missy shook her head. "No, Carla ran into the house-keeper as she was leaving the house, and the house-keeper took a spill down the stairs later," she explained.

"Hmm...am I the only one who thinks that sounds a bit sketchy?" he raised his brows.

"Nice try, Kel, but there's no mystery here. The housekeeper recovered and told police that she had just tripped over one of the dusty old rugs and took a tumble."

"Soooo...yay. Are we going to have any conversation tonight that doesn't revolve around Carla Mayhew?" Echo asked with a tight smile.

"Indeed," Kel nodded. "Enough of boring subjects," he winked at Echo. "What costumes have you fair ladies selected?"

"None yet," Missy sighed. "We don't really know where to go," she lamented.

"Have no fear," the artist directed. "I know just the place. It's a cute little shop, just a couple of towns over. It'll take you maybe 45 minutes to get there, but it's worth the trip. The proprietor is a snippy little vixen name Viviana, who, as rumor would have it..." he looked around and lowered his voice, thrilled with a chance to be dramatic. "Was one of Frederick Palmer's mistresses."

"One of?" Missy asked, shocked. " The Palmers seemed so "old-money conservative.""

"One of many if the rumor mill is to be believed," Kel confirmed. "Why do you think that Blanche is so ready to take him to the cleaners and be on her way?"

"Well, she stormed into my shop not too long ago and seemed very upset because she thought that her husband was having an affair with Carla. Doesn't that mean that she cares about him?"

Kel chuckled. "Oh, my dear...you don't know the history. Freddie-boy and Carla dated in high school, and when he asked her to marry him, she declined. Blanche was his consolation prize, and since he struck it rich in the family business years ago, Carla has fluttered around him like a moth to a flame," he confided smugly. "Blanche hates Carla because she was the one that Frederick actually wanted, but she thought she was too good for him."

Echo took in a deep breath and released it. "Yeah... we're back to Carla again folks," she reminded them.

"Right, sorry. So, we'll definitely check out the costume shop," she told Kel, as she climbed out of the hot tub. "I'm heading upstairs – can't keep my eyes open – you two stay as long as you like, and feel free to help yourself to any of the snacks and wine in the fridge," she instructed, her bare feet slapping against the pool deck.

Chapter 8

*K*el's description of Costumania as being a "cute little shop" was more than a bit misleading. The place was massive, with an elegant storefront and dressing rooms, backed up by what looked like a football field sized warehouse that held every sort of costume imaginable. Missy and Echo were glad that they'd fortified themselves with coffee and cupcakes before venturing out – it looked like they might be there for quite a while.

They flipped through themed racks, giggling at caveman and cat woman suits and catching their breath at glorious Victorian dresses.

"This is so difficult," Echo marveled at the selection. "I don't know whether to go funny or elegant."

"Well, I made up my mind before I came out here that I wanted a costume where Chas could be a handsome prince, and I could be some sort of princess or something. Whatever I find, I want it to sparkle and float and catch the light," Missy said, clearly having given the matter significant thought.

Echo stopped flipping through costumes and stared at her friend. "You really are a hopeless romantic, aren't you?" she asked, shaking her head with a smile.

"To the core," her friend agreed, unashamed. "If I'm dressing up, it's going to be as girlie and pretty as I can find," she resolved.

"What about this one?" the redhead pulled out a light blue satin and chiffon beauty. "It's Cinderella, and it comes with this white rhinestone studded mask and a tiara. What do you think?" she pulled it out and held it up, as Missy caught her breath.

"Oh, my!" she breathed. "It's perfect!" She took the dress gingerly and held it up against herself, looking at it in one of the many full-length mirrors that happened to be nearby.

"Well then go try it on," Echo encouraged, pulling out a lime green harem girl costume. "I think I'm going to try this," she said with a mischievous grin.

"Interesting choice," Missy raised an eyebrow and smiled. "I'm sure Kel will approve," she teased.

"He has nothing to do with this," her friend protested. "I've always wanted to look like the genie on that one 70's TV show," she said, running the silky fabric through her fingers.

"Let's hit the dressing rooms, then," Missy replied, heading toward the front of the store.

Both costumes fit perfectly, and the daring duo decided to celebrate their finds by going out to lunch. When both were stuffed with fresh seafood, they headed back to the inn.

"Hmm...Carla's car is out in front of *Cupcakes in Paradise*," Missy mused when they drove up.

"Makes sense, it's Tuesday," Echo reminded her, making a face. "Ugh. I'll just go straight to my room," she muttered, gathering the large garment bag that held her costume.

"I totally understand, honey, I'll see you later," Missy nodded.

"Here, let me take your costume up," her friend offered, reaching for Missy's bag.

"Thanks, you're a doll," she smiled giving her the bag and a hug. Neither saw the dark glance that Carla cast at the two friends.

"Hey, there," Missy waved when she came up to the driver's side window.

Carla rolled the window down and gave her a pinched smile. "Forget something?" she asked, glancing over at the shop.

"Yes, I did, sorry," she apologized, despite the fact that they hadn't made specific plans to get together. Apparently, Carla had just assumed that Missy would be available every Tuesday. "Do you want to come in for coffee?" she offered, not wanting to seem inhospitable.

Carla looked at her watch and sighed. "No, I can't now. I've been waiting for 45 minutes, and now I have to get going," she said, seeming irritated.

"Okay, well, next time then," Missy agreed, secretly relieved.

"Hey," Carla called out as Missy started to walk away. Missy turned back, a questioning look on her face.

"I just wanted to apologize for what happened at the art show," she said, looking embarrassed. "I think all of the stress that I've been under just came out in an inappropriate way," she explained.

"I know you've been stressed, and I'm sorry that things have been so tough for you," her friend nodded. "But I'm thinking that I'm not the only one who should be hearing this apology," she said gently.

Carla smiled tightly and gave a quick nod. "Yes, well, I've gotta run. Talk to you soon," she said with a dismissive wave and gunned the engine of her car, tearing out into the street while Missy stood, watching her go.

Chapter 9

Missy felt elegant and mysterious as she looked in her full-length mirror after securing her mask.

"You are a stunning Cinderella," Chas smiled, his mouth the only part of his face that showed beneath his mask. He came up behind her, and wrapping his arms around her waist, kissed her neck.

"Well, thank you, my handsome prince," she replied.

"Ready to go?" he asked, taking her hand and twirling her in an impromptu dance move.

"Yes! Let's go get Echo," she answered, her excitement more than evident.

"Wow, look at you!" Missy exclaimed when she saw her friend, who looked exactly like a flame-haired version of the television genie.

"Says the perfect princess," Echo winked. "Let's do this!"

"Your wish is my command, ladies," said Chas, opening their doors with a flourish.

They arrived at the party and Chas handed over his keys to the valet who had been hired for the occasion. The door to the foyer was open, with music and laughter spilling out. Missy was impressed by the job that Carla had done with the interior. Walls which had been disgraced by peeling and stained wallpaper, now featured contemporary geometrics in a subtle palette of greys and blues. Crystal lighting sparkled, and polished wood gleamed in the beautifully restored Victorian.

"Welcome," a large man in a bullfighter's outfit greeted them.

"Missy, this is my boss, Reginald Cho," Chas introduced the man, who shook her hand warmly. "Reggie, this is our very dear friend, Echo Willis."

"Charmed to meet you both," the host smiled graciously, then gestured to the tiny woman in a gypsy outfit, with a veil across her face, who appeared at his side. "This is my lovely wife, Anne."

"Please, make yourselves at home," Anne instructed.

" There is a bar set up in the parlor, lots and lots of goodies to munch on in the dining room, and we have live music in the ballroom. I hope you'll stick around for the costume parade – I think it'll be quite entertaining," she giggled.

The trio thanked their hosts and headed for food and drink. They ran into Kel, looking quite dashing in his Lone Ranger costume, hovering near the hors d'oeuvres.

"Dreams do come true," he teased when he saw Echo and Missy, making Echo blush to the tips of her ears. "I will warn you, dear genie, your nemesis is lurking about somewhere," he said, referring of course to Carla. "She's dressed as a vampire...I could comment further, but, being a gentleman above all else, I shant," he said with a devilish grin.

"Well, she did a great job on the house," Missy observed, in an attempt to be positive.

Kel grimaced a bit. "If you like an un-opinionated and perfectly balanced aesthetic, I suppose it's okay," he shrugged.

Echo snickered and twined her arm through his. "Would you care to dance, Lone Ranger?" she asked from behind her veil.

"I thought you'd never ask," the artist replied with a grin, and they moved off toward the ballroom.

Missy and Chas grinned at each other and watched the two creative souls sashay their way out, headed for the dance floor.

"I promise that I won't pass out in your arms this time, Detective," came a wry voice from behind them. They turned to see Carla, in full vampire splendor.

"No worries," Chas said graciously, putting an arm casually around his wife's waist.

"You two look great," the decorator smiled, looking a bit wistful.

"Thanks, so do you," Missy replied. "And the house is amazing."

"Thanks – Reggie and Anne have great taste, I just put everything together," Carla shrugged modestly.

A woman in a white feathered ball gown with an elaborate swan mask swooped down upon them with an unexpected ferocity.

"Well, well, well, who'd have thought that the Chief would invite the house help to the wedding," sneered Blanche Palmer from behind her mask. Her face was so well hidden that, until she spoke, no one had recognized her, but at the sound of her shrill and rude remark, several heads turned.

Missy cringed at the woman's social impropriety, but Carla's reaction was much more dramatic.

"Really?" the decorator snarled. "Because I wasn't aware that they had invited a card-carrying member of the rejected women's club. Or, did you use the costume to sneak in as one of Freddie's mistresses?"

CRACK! Blanche Palmer slapped Carla so hard in the face that she staggered sideways, holding her cheek.

"You wretched..." the decorator shrieked, charging toward the woman.

Chas stepped in between the two fuming women, surrounded by bosoms heaving in indignation.

"Ladies, please," he held up his hands. "This is a social function, I'd hate to have to arrest someone," he gave them both a pointed look as they continued to glare at each other from opposite sides of the detective. "Now, both of you, turn and walk away, or I'd be happy to take you to the station," he warned.

Blanche was the first to come to her senses. Looking at Carla with utter contempt, she sneered, "You're not even close to worth it."

"You have no idea what you've started," the decorator growled. "You may have started this, but I'll finish it, mark my words, you little..."

"Okay," Chas interrupted. "That's just about enough, Mrs. Mayhew," he said, physically turning Carla around, and marching her from the room.

"Carla, what is it between you and that woman?" Missy whispered, humiliated on behalf of her friend.

"She's hated me ever since she started dating Freddie. He made no secret of the fact that she was his second choice, and I think he regrets ever having married her in the first place," the decorator glared back toward the direction that Blanche had gone.

"Particularly now that you're single?" Missy asked, eyebrow raised.

"What are you trying to say?" Carla gasped. "Wow, I thought in all of the craziness of my life that I had at least one friend that I could count on. Someone who would actually be on my side for a change," she huffed. "But apparently not," she gave Missy a scathing look and headed for the bar.

"Chas," Missy placed her hand on her husband's arm, dismayed.

"Sweetie, there's nothing that we can do. She's a grown woman who makes her own decisions – we can't rescue her every time that she decides to be childish," he said, shaking his head. "Let's just try to forget about what we just witnessed and concentrate on enjoying ourselves. Echo and Kel are on the dance floor, why don't we join them?" he suggested, kissing her forehead.

"Okay," she nodded, feeling bad for Carla, but appalled at the way she'd been acting.

Echo and Kel made quite the fetching couple on the dance floor, moving together gracefully and well, talking and laughing all the while. Missy and Chas joined them, only stopping when they were out of breath and glowing. Chas headed to the punch bowl for some refreshments while the other three sat at a small table, and Missy saw Blanche Palmer cross his path without even acknowledging him. She inclined her head toward Echo to tell her about what had happened, and saw Blanche over her friend's left shoulder, disappearing into an ante-room. Shaking her head, she turned back around to where she had just seen the socialite, wondering how she'd crossed the room so quickly. Kel tugged on her sleeve to get her attention, launching into a hilarious story about an art student, and she forgot all about the snooty woman.

Missy looked for Carla before they left, but apparently the decorator had made the wise decision to leave early, and she felt guilty for feeling relieved. Echo was getting a ride home from Kel, and Missy and Chas were nearly to the front door when a scream ripped through the house.

"Stay here," Detective Chas Beckett instructed his beautiful bride, before sprinting toward the sound. Chief Cho came out moments later and asked everyone who remained at the party to gather in the ballroom, and spoke to some of the officers who were present, giving them instructions in a low voice.

Missy sat with the handful of other guests who were congregating in clumps around the dance floor, speculating as to what might have happened. When Chas came in to find her, she jumped to her feet and searched his eyes.

"Chas, what happened?" she asked fearfully as he steered her subtly from the room.

"There's been a murder," he confided in a low voice. " I know you didn't see anything because we were together the entire night, so I'm going to let you take the car and go. I'll catch a ride from one of the guys when we're done here, but it's going to be a long night. We have to interview every guest," he explained.

"Oh, my goodness," Missy's hands went to her throat. "Who was murdered?"

"We'll talk about it later," he assured her, giving her a quick kiss and guiding her to the door so that she could slip out unnoticed.

Chapter 10

Missy woke up early, to an empty bed, the morning after the masquerade. Chas had been at the Chief's house all night, spearheading the investigation of the murder. She went to the kitchen and poured herself a cup of tea, taking it to the sunporch off of the Master bedroom, tucking her feet underneath her on the sofa. After she finished the tea, she must have dozed off, because the next thing that she knew, the sun was shining in, and Chas was coming through the doorway.

"Morning, beautiful," he greeted her with a kiss. His handsome face bore the signs of extreme fatigue.

"Hey, sweetie," she yawned and stretched. "Did you solve the case?"

"Not yet," he shook his head. "Unfortunately, we have identified a person of interest."

"Why is that unfortunate?" she sat up, curious.

"Because the person of interest is Carla Mayhew," he announced grimly.

Missy's eyes grew wide. "What? Who was the victim?"

"Frederick Palmer," the detective replied.

Missy, Echo and Kel sat at a table in the cupcake shop, munching cupcakes and drinking coffee.

"Wow, so the nasty little decorator finally snapped and offed someone?" Echo asked. "I can't say I'm terribly surprised. You have to admit, her behavior doesn't exactly seem stable. Besides, she has nothing to lose, her son and husband are gone. Maybe she's hoping she'll get caught," she shrugged.

"Echo, that's an awful thing to say. I know Carla may have been rude to you, and even injured you, but I seriously don't think she's the type of person to kill another human being," her friend insisted.

"They usually don't," Kel mused, sipping his coffee.

"Huh? Who doesn't what?" Missy asked, confused.

"Killers don't usually seem the type to kill. Interviews with friends and family members typically say that they never would have seen it coming. On the other hand...why would Carla snuff her potential new meal ticket? It doesn't make sense for her to have killed the man who was reputed to be her lover, particularly since he has more money than the rest of the state of Florida put together."

"Hmm...for someone who was so "happily" married, the rumors about her and other men are rampant aren't they?" Echo observed. Carla's husband had been killed by the ex-police chief, with whom she'd had an affair several years prior. After her husband's death, the chief came calling again, and in her grief, she succumbed to his advances, having no idea that he was her husband's killer. Now, if the rumors were true, she had been seeing the soon-to-be-divorced-but-now-dead Frederick Palmer.

"Glad I'm not always the one who has to point such things out," Kel remarked.

Missy sighed. "We have to get to the bottom of this.

For my own sanity, I have to know whether Carla is innocent or guilty," she admitted.

"Well, have you talked to her since the party?" Echo asked.

"No. She won't return my calls or texts, and when I stopped by a couple of times, she didn't answer the door. I don't know if she was even home."

"Well, where else would she be if her lover is dead?" Echo asked rhetorically. "Doesn't it seem odd that death just seems to follow that woman? I mean, think about it...first her husband...then her son... and now, her lover – doesn't that strike anyone else as being way too much of a coincidence?"

Missy and Kel stared at her, then glanced at each other.

The artist leaned forward conspiratorially. "I know your husband is more than capable of doing his job, but if you're up for it...perhaps we could make his life a bit easier by checking some things out," he proposed with a sly grin.

"I'm in," Echo agreed instantly, then looked at Missy.

"I...don't know," she hesitated. "That sounds like it could be dangerous..."

"Only if your dear friend Carla actually is a black widow," Kel pointed out reasonably. "And you said yourself that you didn't think that was the case," he challenged.

"Well, I am usually pretty good at figuring out who the bad guys are, but I wouldn't even know where to begin," she sighed.

"Why not begin by cozying up to the merry widow?" he suggested. "If she thinks that you're on her side, she may spill her guts, metaphorically speaking."

"To the wife of a detective? Not likely," Missy scoffed.

"If you hang out with her, you may pick up on things just by watching how she reacts. You could maybe see something in her house that would give you a clue. Isn't it worth a shot?" Echo asked. "Don't you think Chas would be happy if you helped solve the case? You've done it plenty of times before," her friend reminded her.

"I suppose so," Missy pursed her lips as her two companions stared at her, awaiting an answer. "Where do we start?"

Chapter 11

*M*issy took a deep breath, then used the hand that wasn't holding a box of Lemon Raspberry cupcakes to ring the doorbell at Carla Mayhew's modest ranch house. As usual, there was no answer. She rang again and waited. Still nothing.

"Carla, honey? It's Missy. I'm worried about you," she called at the door. "I know you don't eat when you're sad, but you need to, so I brought cupcakes," she tried again, knocking after she spoke. She waited a few more seconds, then started to turn to go, when she heard the rasp of the chain lock being slid back.

Carla opened the door maybe six inches. "The house is a mess," said the disheveled creature in the darkened house.

"Oh, sweetie, I don't care about that," Missy assured her. "I can help you clean it if you want me to," she offered.

"No," Carla murmured, looking down at the floor.

"You look like you need a hug," Missy said softly, nudging the door open a bit with her free hand. The decorator cried silently, fat tears running down her cheeks, her shoulders shaking. She opened the door and Missy came in, setting the cupcakes down on a hall table. She went to the clearly distraught woman and embraced her warmly, cooing to her like one would to a child.

"Okay...it's okay...you just let it out," she whispered, smoothing down Carla's rat's nest hair that looked and smelled as though she hadn't bathed since the party. She had lost weight, her shoulders and waist felt thin as Missy held her. They stood swaying in the front hall for several minutes, Carla crying and Missy soothing. Finally, the decorator pulled back, suddenly embarrassed, wiping her eyes and nose with the sleeve of the colorless grey sweatshirt that hung on her frame like rags on a scarecrow.

"You poor dear," Missy said, her sympathy genuine. "Let's sit you down and I'll make us some tea. When is the last time you had something to eat?"

Carla shrugged. "I don't remember. I don't get hungry anymore," she said dully, sitting in the chair that Missy pulled out for her at the kitchen island. The top of the island was so cluttered that Missy couldn't even see it, so once she put the teakettle on, she began methodically clearing it, putting dishes in the dishwasher, though there were few, mail in the bin to be sorted, and miscellaneous items wherever it seemed they needed to be. She had the entire top cleared, wiped down and set with two plates, napkins and silverware before the kettle whistled.

"Is there anything in the house to eat?" Missy asked, opening the refrigerator and noting with dismay that most of the items in there looked expired and inedible. There was a stench that nearly made her gag, so she started taking out anything that was moldy or expired, and stuffing it into the garbage can so that she could take it out.

"Probably not," Carla mumbled, her head in her hands.

Pausing in her effort to rid the refrigerator of its potentially toxic contents, she pulled her phone out of her back pocket and hit #3 on her speed dial list.

"Maggie? Hi. Listen, I need a favor if you could..." she gave the innkeeper instructions as to what food to pack and how to get to Carla's house, then went back to cleaning.

"Help is on the way. We're going to get some decent food in you before we indulge in cupcakes," she informed the depressed woman. "Here's your tea. I put a little bit of honey in it to make you feel a little bit better. I'm guessing that your blood sugar is a bit low, so this should give you a little boost. Drink up," she counseled, sitting down next to the forlorn creature.

"Did Chas send you to try to get information from me?" she asked, not looking at Missy.

"No. He'd actually probably be upset if he knew I had come, but I had to see how you're doing. I've been worried about you, especially when you didn't answer my calls or texts," she replied.

"I didn't want to see anyone," the decorator admitted, her voice barely audible. "I've felt people looking at me funny ever since Roger died, and lately it's gotten worse. Now they think I'm a murderer," she started crying again, her head hanging between her hands, elbows on the counter.

Missy handed her the cup of tea, and she took a couple of sips, then put the cup down again. "Sweetie, if you didn't do anything wrong, you don't have anything to worry about," she said, reaching for Carla's hand and patting it.

"If? If I've done nothing wrong? You don't even believe that I'm innocent, and you're supposed to be my friend. My only friend, these days," she accused.

Missy bristled. "Do you honestly think I'd come over here to make sure that you were okay if I thought for one second that you were a murderer? Come on, I know you're hurting, but that's just silly," she said, her tone softening. She had a brief pang of conscience, knowing that she had indeed wondered if Carla was a killer before she came over. In fact, she still thought it might be a possibility, but needed to talk to her more before she could be sure.

"Let's get some food into you, maybe go for a walk, and just try to get you feeling a little bit better, okay? I can't stand seeing you so upset," Missy confessed. This was actually true, she hated to see anyone, or anything suffer, and if there was something that she could do to prevent it, she'd try her best. Maggie arrived in short order, handing over roasted chicken, fingerling potatoes, steamed green beans, a freshly tossed Caesar salad, and a jar of Missy's homemade ham and bean soup. Missy put the soup in the pantry so that Carla would have something easy to heat up later, then fixed them plates of wholesome, homemade food. The decorator nibbled on a succulent potato, shining with a touch of butter, and tinged with the slightest flavor of garlic, and started crying again.

"What's wrong?" Missy asked, putting down her fork.

"I've been so mean to you, and you're never anything but nice to me. I've avoided you and been snippy with you, and you just give me cupcakes and make me tea and bring me food," she blubbered.

"Well, honey, where I come from, that's what friends do for one another. What kind of friend would I be if I ditched you because you're having a bad day, or a series of bad days, or said something unkind? You just dry those tears and eat some of Maggie's good cooking," she ordered. "You'll be feeling better in no time."

The two women got down to the business of eating, and much to Missy's amazement, Carla ate most of the food on her plate before pushing it away with a happy groan.

"See? It worked, didn't it?" Missy smiled.

"Yeah, I actually do feel a lot better," the decorator

admitted.

"Chicken is good for the soul. Ready for a cupcake, or should we save those for later?"

"Later," Carla replied, holding up a hand. "I can't possibly put one more thing in this tummy," she patted her midsection. "Thank you, Missy. I know I've been difficult, and it really means a lot to me that you're still my friend," she said softly.

"Of course I'm still your friend," Missy said, moving in for a hug. "Ready for a walk?" She wanted to get Carla out of the house for some fresh air and exercise. She'd apparently been cooped up in her house for days.

"I...don't know. What if someone sees me and says something nasty?" she worried.

"I'll tell them where they can go and precisely how to get there," Missy said, raising her eyebrows to show she meant business.

One corner of the decorator's mouth actually crooked upward into a semblance of a smile. "Okay, I'll give it a shot," she agreed.

"I'm really sad about Frederick," Carla confided, once they were outside. "We weren't having an affair, but since we got reacquainted, we had the best talks. He wasn't happy in his marriage. Apparently, Blanche is a cold fish, so he was starving for attention and affection."

"And you gave him both," Missy supplied, without judgment.

"Exactly, but it was completely platonic. It was like having a really sweet brother to talk to. He'd talk about his dying marriage and I'd talk about my dead husband and son and the mistake that I'd made in having an affair. Neither one of us had to pretend, and neither one of us judged the other. It was comfortable and easy and fun," she finished sadly.

"No wonder I didn't see as much of you. Someone had replaced me as your confidant," Missy teased.

"No one could ever replace you, but Freddie knew me from the old days, you know? He knew me before I was old and jaded – back when I had hopes and dreams – shared history can be very powerful."

"Oh, believe me, I know," Missy nodded. "I felt like a huge part of my heart had died when I left Louisiana. Everyone I'd ever known, every memory I'd ever had, was in that sweet small town."

"So, obviously, there's no way I would've killed my best friend from high school," Carla offered reasonably.

"Obviously," Missy agreed, glad that the decorator had brought it up so that she didn't have to. "But, who do you think did it?" she asked, working very hard to keep her tone casual.

"Well, as far as I know, the only person who would stand to profit from Freddie's death would be his wretched wife, Blanche," Carla gritted her teeth. "If he died before they could sign divorce papers, there'd be no need to reach a settlement, because the estate would transfer to her, I would imagine. They never had any kids, although Freddie had an adorable little Pomeranian named Polly," she smiled fondly. "He loved that dog."

"Do you really think that Blanche was hard-hearted enough to kill her husband?"

"I think that she thought that Freddie wanted to marry me after the divorce, and she'd do whatever she had to in order to make sure that I didn't eventually receive what she thought of as hers," Carla theorized.

"Freddie?"

"Freddie's money," the decorator said bitterly. "That's all she wanted all along. She was dating someone else when Freddie and I broke up in high school, and she dumped her current boyfriend in order to chase him. His family had money, and she desperately wanted to improve her social standing. Unfortunately, Freddie fell for her sickly sweetness and married the shrew."

"That's so sad," Missy said. "So, he was actually a good guy? I've heard things about his...extramarital activities," she said, hoping that Carla wouldn't be offended.

"Well, for one thing, you've got to stop listing to that

drama queen, Phillip Kellerman," the decorator shook her head and smiled another half-smile. "He means well...I think. He got it right this time around though. Yes, Freddie had side action going on. He and Blanche hadn't been intimate in years – she refused him long enough that eventually he just stopped asking. It was kind of an unwritten rule between them that he could have his mistresses as long as he didn't acknowledge them or embarrass Blanche by being seen with them in public. She was fine with that arrangement, until she thought that he actually had someone that he cared about."

"You?" Missy asked.

"Me," Carla nodded. "She didn't worry about mistresses, because she would still get all of the money and benefits of being his wife, but when we rekindled our friendship, she saw her fiscal future threatened. I guess you could say indirectly that I was responsible for Freddie's death if you look at it from that perspective. She wouldn't have killed him if I hadn't come along," she murmured.

"Oh, stop," Missy admonished. "There's no way anyone could've predicted anything like this."

"Yeah, I suppose you're right," Carla agreed, still morose. "I think we should head back now," she said, shivering. "I'm starting to get cold."

"Well, we can't have that," Missy put an arm around the tiny woman's shoulders, rubbing her upper arm to warm her up as they turned to go back to her house. "We'll get you back inside and I'll run a nice hot bath for you."

"Mmmm...a bath sounds lovely," Carla nodded, weary after having walked and talked for so long after not having been active for days.

Chapter 12

"I'm sorry, I just don't think she did it," Missy told Echo and Kel over coffee and freshly baked croissants the next morning.

"Well, no offense girlie, but you are known for always trying to see the best in people," Echo gave her a pointed look.

"It's nice to give folks the benefit of the doubt, but she disappeared from the party early, and has no alibi. She'd also had a fight with Frederick at his house the day before the party because Blanche wanted to pull the funding for her interior decorating project," Kel asserted.

"Wait...how could you possibly know that?" Missy challenged the artist.

"I get my pedicures at the same salon as the Palmer's housekeeper, Carmelita. She witnessed the whole thing," he shrugged.

Missy's face fell. She wondered why, if Carla had been telling the truth, she hadn't mentioned the fight over her interior decorating job being terminated.

"So, can you see how it might be plausible that Carla could've killed Frederick Palmer?" Echo asked.

"I'm so confused right now," Missy said. "I don't think we're getting the whole picture here."

"Too bad you can't ask your hubby for a little insider info..." Kel mused.

"Definitely not. I'm not going to ask Chas to divulge information from an ongoing investigation – it could cost him his job," she shook her head vehemently.

"Just a thought," the artist held up his hands in mock-surrender. "We can brainstorm some more tomorrow. As of right now, you have a customer coming in," he observed, gazing over her shoulder at the door.

"Duty calls," Echo said, standing and gathering cups and plates. She moved behind the counter and put the dirty dishes in the kitchen while Missy stood at the register and greeted the twenty-something Barbie look-alike who had just alighted from a very expensive sports car. Kel stayed at the table and nodded politely to the woman when she breezed into the shop. She was dressed in a warmup suit that probably cost nearly as much as the car, and had perfect teeth, breasts, hair and nails. All had elements of artificiality, but she wore them well.

"Hi, how may I help you?" Missy asked.

"Okay, I want a cupcake that is sugar-free, fat-free, and gluten-free, and I'm in a hurry," the high-maintenance blonde said through her nose.

"Well, I have sugar-free, fat-free, or gluten-free, but I don't have anything that encompasses all three requests, I'm afraid. Sorry," Missy said. "Would you like some coffee?"

"Are you serious?" the woman looked at her with unconcealed disdain. When Missy merely blinked at her, she sighed loudly. "Fine. I'll take a sugar-free soy caramel latte, heated to 120 degrees," she said, examining her nails.

"Sorry, we don't do specialty drinks. When I said coffee, I literally meant a cup of coffee. We have cream and sugar if you'd like. There's also tea," Missy explained, rapidly losing patience.

"Wow, this is unbelievable," the Barbie complained. "Fine. Give me a Chai tea, with..."

"We only have tea bags and hot water," Missy interrupted her before she could go into yet another detailed and particular order.

The young woman stared at her for a moment, shaking her head. "Unreal." She looked in the display case which had been there in front of her the entire time and finally came to a realistic decision. "Give me one of those chocolate coconut thingies in the front then, and it had better not make me sick or I'll sue," she threatened, reaching into her designer bag for her wallet. The wallet was stuffed to the gills with hundred-dollar bills.

"That'll be $3.80," Missy said, and Barbie handed her a hundred. "I'm sorry, I don't have change for a one-hundred-dollar bill, do you have anything smaller?" she said handing the bill back to the irritated blonde.

"No, I don't have anything smaller," she seemed stunned. "Do you honestly mean to tell me that I'm going to have to give you a Carte Blanche for three dollars and eighty cents?" she demanded.

"Well, no, actually, my machine doesn't accept Carte Blanche, do you have a different card?" Missy asked sweetly, as Kel, who had been watching the entire exchange, tried to conceal his chuckle with a cough.

"What about you, Pops?" she asked rudely, whirling to face Kel. "Do *you* have change for a hundred?"

"Starving artist, I'm afraid," he grinned, shrugging.

With a loud sigh, she turned back to Missy and again tried to hand her a hundred-dollar bill. Missy refused it again.

"I'm sorry, I can't take it. I don't have that kind of change," she explained, trying desperately to hold on to her civility.

"Take it and keep the stupid change," Barbie yelled, throwing the bill on the counter and snatching the bag with her cupcake out of Missy's hand.

"I can't accept that kind of tip," the shop owner protested.

"Try," the young woman tossed flippantly over her shoulder as she power-walked to the door.

"Oh, my," Missy said, shaking her head, when the

woman had gone. "She seemed familiar somehow," she mused.

"Well, aren't you the perceptive one?" Kel remarked, his raised eyebrows a sure sign that he was impressed.

"What do you mean? Do you know her?"

"I know of her..." he said cryptically.

"So, who is she?" Echo asked, coming out from behind the counter, having observed the interaction from the hall.

"That was one of Frederick Palmer's mistresses. He definitely had a preferred type," the artist chuckled.

"She looks like a younger version of Blanche!" Missy realized.

"Bingo, you get the prize," Kel teased.

"Wow, she was tossing around some serious money for a mistress. What does she do for a living?" Echo asked.

"She owns the costume shop that I sent you to."

Chapter 13

Missy was troubled as she took her morning walk along the beach. There was a cool breeze and she pulled her sweater more tightly around her, but enjoyed the silky feel of the sand on her bare feet. Carla had seemed so sincere when she had gone to see her, but so many things pointed toward her guilt – she just didn't know what to think. She wanted to find out the truth, not only to exact justice for an innocent dead man, but for her own peace of mind. If the decorator was truly a killer, Missy was worried for Echo's safety, because Carla clearly had a grudge against her. What if she actually had been in on her own husband's death? The former police chief had insisted he hadn't killed Roger Mayhew, but fell short of placing the blame on the deceased's wife.

The tender-hearted cupcake shop owner's stomach churned at the thought. She hadn't slept well, and knew that her rest would be broken until she found out the truth. She'd talk to Echo and Kel today and strategize about what to do next.

Echo was enjoying breakfast with the other guests of the inn when Chas came in, looking rather stressed.

"Can I talk to you for a minute?" he asked, seeming distracted.

"Sure, I can take my muffin with me," she said, rising from her chair, glass of tomato juice in one hand, a vegan Morning Glory muffin in the other. She followed Chas into an adjoining parlor, and he shut the door behind them for privacy. "What's up?" she asked, taking a bite of muffin.

"I hate to ask, but, where were you around eight o'clock last night?" the detective looked at her intently.

"I was here, watching chick flicks and eating popcorn with Maggie. We started the first movie around seven, and I think the second one was around nine. I went upstairs to bed after that one, neither one of us could keep our eyes open. Why do you ask?"

"Carla Mayhew was attacked last night."

"Wow. She's suspected of killing another woman's husband and you come question me? Seriously? What's up with that, Chas?" she demanded, astonished.

"We just have to chase down all possibilities. Blanche Palmer had an alibi, so we had to look at other options. You've had some very unpleasant public encounters with Carla, so naturally, you were on the list," the detective explained.

"So now you're going to go verify my story with Maggie," she presumed.

Chas nodded. "Standard procedure."

Echo sighed. "It's okay, I get it. How is she?"

"Carla? She's fine. Shaken up, had some stitches, but she'll be okay."

"That's good. Even though she seems to be a vile human being, I never wish harm on others."

Chas looked at her thoughtfully for a moment. "Missy seems to think she's a decent person...but the more I encounter her, the more I wonder..."

"Well, she's certainly not on my favorites list," Echo replied dryly.

The detective switched gears. "Have you seen my lovely wife?" he asked.

"No, but my guess is that if she's not on the sunporch with her coffee, she's probably walking the beach."

"That sounds about right," Chas smiled. "Thanks Echo, I'll see you later." He left the parlor, headed for the beach.

The shape of a person in the distance looked familiar and Missy squinted her eyes to confirm that it was indeed her husband walking toward her.

"Good morning," she greeted him, snuggling into his hug.

"Good morning, Beautiful," he returned, kissing the top of her head. "I need to talk to you about something."

"Uh oh...am I in trouble?"

"Quite possibly," he deadpanned, teasing.

"What's up?" Missy asked, her curiosity getting the best of her.

"You went to visit Carla yesterday," he said simply.

The look on her face was a dead giveaway. "I had to make sure she was okay," she shrugged, unashamed. "But how did you find out about that?"

"Carla told me when I questioned her at the hospital."

"The hospital?" Missy exclaimed. "Why was she at the hospital?" she whispered, hoping that the distraught woman had not tried to harm herself.

"She was attacked in her home last night as she was about to get into the tub," Chas explained.

"What??? That had to have been right after I left! I started the bath water for her," she was wide-eyed.

"That's what Carla said," he nodded. "The theory is that whoever attacked her, slipped into the bathroom behind her, because the water running would cover any sounds, and knocked her feet out from under her, causing her to hit her head on the side of the tub when she fell. She was knocked unconscious and the fall caused the skin just above her temple to split open. Head wounds tend to bleed pretty badly, so she lost some blood, but when she regained consciousness, she called 911."

"Oh, my, that's awful, poor thing," Missy murmured.

"Yeah, she can't seem to catch a break. So now we're looking into who might've done such a thing, and the two primary candidates both have air-tight alibis," he shook his head in frustration.

"Blanche and Echo?"

"Yep. Any ideas who else might want to hurt her?" he asked.

"Not a clue, but I can talk to her later about it if you'd like," she offered.

"Give it a shot," he shrugged. "But make it conversational. This isn't official in any way," he warned. "I've questioned her at length, but apparently she trusts you, so maybe she'll confide in you."

"Maybe," Missy murmured, more confused than ever.

Chapter 14

"I still think that Carla is innocent," Missy insisted as she, Kel and Echo devoured their breakfast at *Cupcakes in Paradise*.

"Fine. But if she's innocent, who killed Frederick Palmer?" Echo challenged.

"My bet would be on his "dear" wife," Kel interjected, wiping crumbs from his mouth with a tiny napkin.

"That's my thought too," Missy agreed.

"Fine," Echo sighed. "But how do we go about finding out?"

"I may actually have an idea about that," Kel smiled slyly.

"Do tell," the feisty redhead replied, warming her hands on her coffee cup.

"Well, as it turns out, I have a friend of a friend who has a cousin in the coroner's office," he leaned in, speaking in a low voice, despite the fact that no one else was in the shop. "And it just happened to get back to me through the grapevine that old Freddie was killed with a sharp instrument of some kind," he finished smugly.

"Wow, I'm married to the detective on the case and I

didn't know that," Missy shook her head. "So...how does that help us?"

"Sharp instruments cause trauma, which causes blood...lots of it. The Chief's housekeeper said it took them hours to scrub away the stains on the cloakroom floor, but I digress. If there is blood involved, wouldn't it be logical to assume that there might be blood on the costume of the person who murdered Freddie?" he asked, as light dawned for Missy and Echo.

"So, all we have to do is go rent the costume that Blanche wore, and check it for blood stains!" Echo exclaimed.

"Amateur," Kel teased, shaking his head and clucking his tongue. "If we rent the costume, and the deceased's blood is found on it, we can potentially implicate ourselves in some kind of wrongdoing. We merely need to go looking at costumes and check the one in question for blood stains in the process. We take a photo, call the police and go on our merry way," he explained.

"How do you even think of those things?" Echo asked, impressed.

"I read a lot of mysteries," he winked.

"There may be a snag in your plan," Missy said, turning over various scenarios in her mind.

"Oh?" Kel looked skeptical.

"Yes, hang on," she said, pulling her phone out of her back pocket. She went to a search engine, found the information that she was searching for, and hit 'Dial' on the web page.

"Hello, I have a question – do you launder the

costumes when they are returned, or should I do that before I bring it back?" she asked the young woman who answered the phone. She listened for a moment, then replied. "Oh, I have to dry clean it? Okay, thanks so much."

"Well, aren't you the clever one," Kel remarked with admiration. "Do you read mysteries too?"

"My whole life is a series of mysteries," she sighed, then got back to the business at hand. "So, if Blanche had the costume dry-cleaned, any evidence might be erased," she frowned.

"Not necessarily," the artist replied. "As one whose entire wardrobe is dry-clean only, I can tell you on good authority, that if a blood stain is not specifically pointed out and marked to be treated, it will most likely be overlooked and set in permanently during the dry-cleaning process."

"Or...Blanche may have done what most people do and just pinned an old dry-cleaning tag on it to say that it had been cleaned, even if it hadn't," Echo suggested practically.

"The very idea," Kel exclaimed, appalled.

"Hey, those chemicals are very bad for the environment," she shot back. "You're probably absorbing all sorts of toxins on a daily basis," she frowned.

"I don't do laundry, I'll take my chances," the artist sniffed.

"We can solve global warming another day, kids – can we please just focus here for a minute?" Missy admonished.

"Quite right," Kel agreed. "Shall we head to the costume shop, then?"

"Go for it," Echo said. "I'll take care of things here, and you guys come tell me everything when you get back."

"Will do," said Missy, reaching in her purse for car keys.

Chapter 15

"Now, whatever you do, act natural," Kel muttered as he and Missy walked to the front door of Costumania.

"Why did you have to say that?" she hissed back. "Now I'm going to feel weird and awkward."

"Welcome to my world, darling," the artist patted her shoulder.

The bells at the top of the door jangled loudly in the nearly-empty costume shop, and the same young girl who had been manning the cash register when Missy and Echo came in to shop, greeted them pleasantly.

"Hi, can I help you find something?" she asked.

"Hello," Kel's voice boomed through the store. "I'm having an exhibit featuring art inspired by nature and I need to look at animal costumes, particularly flying animals...bats, birds, butterflies...if you could point us in the direction of that particular section, we'd be most appreciative," he asked, ever the gentleman.

"Sure, come with me," the girl smiled and led the way through the warehouse.

"Wow, you're really good at this sort of thing," Missy whispered in admiration.

"Acting is a form of art, my lovely," he replied with a sly grin.

"Thank you so much, dear," he bowed slightly to the young woman, who left them with instructions to "holler if you need anything."

The dynamic duo made a beeline to a clump of white feathers that they saw sticking out of the row of bird costumes, and found the swan dresses and masks almost immediately.

"There are two of them," Kel observed.

"Then we'll check them both," Missy decreed, grabbing the first dress and leaving Kel the other.

"Here it is," she said, holding a piece of the skirt up in triumph. "There's blood on the hem of this one," she whispered excitedly. "It doesn't look like it was even taken to the dry cleaner, these are pretty dramatic." She snapped a quick picture with her phone.

"Umm...I do believe this mystery has just gotten significantly more complicated," the artist mused, focusing on the dress he was holding.

"What makes you say that?"

"There's blood on this one too," he replied, holding up some of the feathers on the skirt to reveal the undeniable stains. He photographed the evidence for future reference.

"How could that be?" Missy wondered.

"Looks to me like Ms. Blanche had an accomplice," Kel raised an eyebrow.

"I knew it!" she exclaimed, startling the artist. "I thought that I saw Blanche in two different places at once during the party. She and her accomplice must've accidentally crossed paths with each other. But who would be crazy enough to participate in a murder with her?" asked a very baffled Missy.

"Let's forget about who for the moment and think about how," he advised, heading for the front of the store.

"Wait, where are you going?" Missy asked, jogging to keep up with his lengthy stride.

"To the accessories counter, where else?"

"Huh?"

"Trust me, my dear," he said, cryptically.

"Hello, lovely lady," Kel greeted the cashier. "One of the swan costumes took my associate's fancy," he said, gesturing to Missy. "Is there a particular set of accessories that you'd recommend for it? We're looking for something rather elegant."

"Well, they were both rented out recently, and one of the ladies used our swan ring as one of the accessories. I don't see it here, but, let me check and see if it came back with the dress. I'll be right back," she promised.

"What are you looking for?" Missy whispered, when the young woman was out of sight.

"The murder weapon, my dear. From what I hear, it wasn't recovered at the scene, and the wound was quite unique...it was triangular in shape," he whispered back. Missy wanted to ask him how he knew all of that, but they heard the young woman's footsteps and broke apart, pretending to peruse the items in the accessories case.

"Apparently, it didn't come back in with the costume," the woman frowned. "I'm sorry about that."

Undaunted, as always, Kel persisted. "Oh, what a pity. Do you have a photo of it, so that perhaps we can order one?"

"Oh, that's a great idea," the cashier brightened. "I can show it to you in our catalog," she offered.

"Perfect," Kel beamed.

Missy had to force herself to stand still while the young woman flipped through several pages of a giant catalog, searching for the ring. She hoped that they weren't just spinning their wheels by pursuing Kel's hunch.

"Ah, here we go," she exclaimed, turning the book toward Missy and Kel. The ring was stunning, featuring an elegant swan, whose neck twined around the finger, and whose wings came to a graceful, triangular point over the back of the hand. The two exchanged a knowing glance.

"I love it," Missy nodded, taking her acting cue from Kel. "That's the one, when we come back to finalize our rental, we'll order that too. Do you mind if I take a photo of it? I think he might be inspired to create a piece of art that will pay homage to this ring," she confided, smiling at Kel.

"Of course, no problem," the cashier replied. "Go right ahead."

"Do you happen to know the size of the one that's gone missing?" the artist asked pleasantly. "If it's the right size and it comes back in before we reserve the costume, we may not have to order another one," he explained.

"Let me just check," she offered, opening up the ledger of rental receipts. Again, she flipped through several pages until she found the nearly identical reservations side by side. Running her finger down the inventory of items, she found the notation for the ring. "Here we go," she said again. She glanced at Missy's hand. "It might just fit you, since you have tiny fingers. It's a size five and a half," she informed them, closing the book, but not before Kel had taken a good, long look at the order.

"Well, there we have it," he grinned. "Thank you so much for your time, dear lady. We shall return."

"Well, that was certainly a wealth of information," Missy mused, once they were in the car.

"More so than you think," Kel replied with a smirk.

"What do you mean?"

"While our dear helper was busy looking at your hand, I was busy looking at the ledger. Blanche Palmer didn't rent those two dresses," he smiled like a Cheshire cat.

"What? But...Blanche was wearing the dress...I saw her. If she didn't rent them, who did?" Missy asked, wide-eyed.

Chapter 16

"Are you trying to tell me that the prissy little princess who came into the store the other day is the mastermind behind Frederick Palmer's death?" Missy demanded in disbelief.

"She's certainly the one who reserved both of the costumes that weekend. Blanche's name was nowhere to be found, and I would assume that's because she didn't want there to be any record of her having been in contact with Viviana Mason, her husband's current mistress," Kel shrugged.

"Can I just make the observation that this guy was nowhere near hot enough to be having all of these affairs with attractive women?" Echo remarked, lightening the mood. Kel chuckled and Missy sighed.

"Why would she do that?" Missy challenged the artist.

"Did you happen to notice how much money she was carrying, what kind of car she was driving and the clothing that she was wearing?" he asked. "Those things cost far more money than Viviana would make in the next ten years running her little costume shop. My guess would be that Blanche made her do the dirty work for a cut of the insurance money."

Missy nodded. "They both probably thought that he was going to marry Carla, leaving them with no funding, so they decided to kill him off and divide the spoils," she deduced. "But, why wouldn't they just kill Carla, rather than Freddie?"

"Because, my dear, if he were alive, he'd still control the money, and what if he found someone else? They had to eliminate him before he divorced Blanche, so that she'd be the sole beneficiary. Besides, if Carla had come up dead, Blanche would have been the obvious suspect and Freddie would've spent his last dime making sure that she was caught and prosecuted," Kel theorized. "And it goes without saying that most wealthy folk are worth far more dead than alive – I'm sure he was insured for millions, if not billions."

"I wonder if they've received the insurance money yet," Echo murmured.

"Doubtful, these things usually take a while, but I have a friend in Freddie's lawyer's office who might be able to take a peek at a file or two," he grinned wickedly.

"Goodness, Kel, do you know everyone in this town?" Missy asked, amazed.

"Pretty much," he nodded. "The more people I know, the more art I sell."

"So now what do we do?" Missy asked, mumbling more to herself than addressing the other two.

"Now, you two hold tight, and I'm going to put a plan into motion that should give us everything we need," he promised with a mysterious smile.

Missy suddenly sat up straight, her eyes wide.

"What is it?" Echo asked, alarmed.

"Carla could be in danger, and while I know that she's not your favorite person, understandably, I should probably go and check on her, now that we think we know who killed Frederick Palmer."

Kel nodded. "Yes, do that. You may even get lucky enough to catch Blanche or Viviana in the act of trying to harm her again. In the meantime, I'm going to gather the info that I need, and hopefully we'll soon have enough to give your husband so that a warrant can be issued."

"I'll mind the store," Echo volunteered. "Although I'm really going to have to start working out if I don't lay off of the cupcakes soon," she moped.

"I wouldn't worry about that just yet," the artist replied, giving her a look that made her blush.

"On that note," Missy said, making a face. "I'm off to Carla's. If you don't hear from me in a couple of hours, come find me," she directed, not knowing what she might be facing.

Chapter 17

*M*issy could feel that something was wrong when she pulled up to Carla's house. There wasn't anything specific that she could put her finger on, but when she stopped the car, she caught a glimpse of a figure in dark clothing darting around the back corner of the home. She got out carefully, not making a sound, pushing the car door shut as gently as she could, and wincing at the click when it closed. She ducked down behind the little maroon car, making sure that her feet were behind the tire so that if whoever it was behind the house glanced over, they'd see no one. Waiting there for a couple of minutes to catch her breath and slow her heart rate, she decided to throw caution to the wind and follow the person.

Running quickly and silently across the street, glad that she had worn her athletic shoes, she crouched behind Carla's car in the driveway, listening. Hearing nothing, she darted between the house and a clump of bushes that led to the back yard, hoping that she wouldn't encounter the intruder just yet. She figured that, if the person in dark clothing was either Viviana or Blanche, she had enough martial arts training and adrenaline to hold her own.

Back against the brick exterior wall, trying desperately to control her breathing, and quite certain that the pounding of her heart could be heard for miles, Missy inched slowly along toward the rear of the building, taking care not to step on any twigs or leaves that would give her away. When she finally made it to the corner, she heard the distinct sound of metal clinking against metal. Holding her breath, she got as close to the building as was physically possible and peeked quickly around the corner. All she saw was dark clothing, blonde hair, and someone who was quite obviously trying to pry open a window. It could be either Viviana or Blanche, which meant that she was going to have to face the situation, rather than slipping away to call the police. Besides, she didn't want to take the chance that whoever it was would get inside while she was calling for help, so she took a deep breath, got ready to dash toward the intruder, and screamed when her ears were suddenly assaulted by a shrill noise.

The alarm system that Carla had installed after being attacked the first time had done its job, startling the intruder as well as Missy, and while the sound had the woman off guard, Missy charged around the corner at full speed, blindsiding her as she attempted to flee. She tackled tiny little Viviana to the ground, flipped her over and secured her arms behind her back before the former mistress had any inkling as to what was happening. Carla opened her back-patio door and saw Missy sitting on top of the intruder.

"Your alarm isn't malfunctioning, this is real – call the police," she ordered, wrestling with the struggling young woman. Carla ran back into the house to call, and came out moments later, still on the phone with the dispatcher, and carrying a roll of duct tape. She helped Missy secure Viviana's hands and feet with the duct tape, then sat with her friend while she restrained the young woman.

Chas was the first one on the scene, and the look on his face when he came around the corner and saw his wife sitting on the suspect was priceless. "I should have known," he raised a disapproving eyebrow.

"It's okay, I'm fine," Missy assured him, as two uniformed patrol officers took over securing the prisoner.

"Weapon," a female officer announced, after patting Viviana down. She extracted from the pocket of the intruder's designer warmups the same ring that had been used to kill Frederick Palmer. Missy shuddered when she saw it.

"That's the ring that killed Frederick Palmer," she

whispered, when Chas came over to inspect her for injury. She was scraped and bruised, but otherwise fine.

"And just how do you know that?" he asked, with a heavy sigh.

"It's a long story..."

He was about to say something when Missy's phone went off in her pocket. She was glad that it hadn't happened earlier, when she had been sneaking up on Viviana. It was Kel, so she answered it. After speaking with him for a few minutes, she handed the phone to her husband.

"Here, honey, you need to hear this," she said as he took the phone with a puzzled frown.

Chapter 18

"You know I'm totally against violence in all forms," Echo prefaced her statement. "But oh, my gosh, you went all Rambo on the little yoga queen? That's amazing," her face beamed with admiration.

"I didn't want Carla to get hurt, and Viviana is just a tiny thing, so I took my chances," Missy shrugged. "What Kel did was much more impressive."

"Oh, really? What did you do? It'll take a lot to top Missy's ninja moves," she teased the artist.

"Oh, it wasn't much, really," he demurred modestly.

"Yes, it was too," Missy insisted. "If he won't say it, I will. He talked to some people that he knew at the bank and found out that, not only had Blanche Palmer withdrawn one hundred thousand dollars from her personal account, but Viviana had made a deposit in that same amount, on the same day."

"So, Blanche paid her to kill Frederick and didn't cover her tracks? That wasn't very smart," Echo mused.

"And that isn't all. Apparently, Freddie had been paying for his mistress's condo, car and wardrobe for quite some time," Kel informed them, eyebrows raised.

"Wow, Blanche and Viviana were both taking him for a ride, weren't they?" Echo shook her head.

"Yep," Missy confirmed. "But it gets better. As it turns out, they killed poor Freddie for nothing. When they were married, he had made Blanche the sole benefi-ciary of all of his insurance policies and his entire estate, but when he realized that there was no saving their marriage and that they were both becoming more and more miserable, he went in to see his attorney, and changed his will," she grinned.

"Do tell," a slow smile spread across Echo's face.

"Well, it seems that Freddie's beloved Pomeranian, Polly, received the entire estate. She is to live out her life in his mansion, to be cared for by the staff. Upon her death, all of his insurance money and his liqui-dated estate will be donated to Florida State No-Kill Shelter Association," Missy couldn't contain her glee.

"Hahahaha! That's poetic," Echo laughed, as did Kel. "They may have killed him, but he still swung the last blow – good for him. It's not like they'll need the money anyway. I would imagine they're going to be in prison for a very, very long time."

"As it should be," Kel intoned grimly.

"Indeed," Missy nodded.

Chapter 19

"It's crazy," Carla said as she and Missy lazed by the pool at the Inn. "One would think that after all of the things that have happened in my life lately, I'd have to move out of town and change my name to get a brand-new start, but the opposite has been true. My phone has been ringing off the hook with new clients."

"People are funny," Missy replied, eyes closed as she soaked up the sun. "Maybe they can see that you were just a victim of circumstance," she proposed.

"Or maybe they just like working with the notorious "black widow decorator," she chuckled.

"Either way, it works out," Missy laughed.

"Good afternoon, ladies," a male voice came from behind their loungers.

Both of them looked up in surprise to see a model-handsome, tanned young man, who looked to be in his late twenties, coming toward them, bearing a tray with two cocktails.

"Hello," Missy said, mystified, wondering if it was Carla's birthday and someone had sent an entertainer.

"Oh, my," Carla breathed.

The man smiled, breaking out in dimples. His

shoulder length, wavy jet-black hair shone in the sun, and his blue eyes were the color of a stormy sea.

"Miss Maggie said that you might be thirsty, so she sent me out here with cocktails for you," he explained, setting the tray down on the small table between their loungers. "I hope you like gin and tonic," he grinned, flashing perfectly white teeth.

"Uh, yes, it's one of my favorite drinks, but...I don't believe we've met," she said, puzzled at the appearance of this gorgeous man.

"Oh, sorry," he said, handing her and Carla their drinks, then wiping his hands on his snugly-fitting khaki shorts. "I'm Spencer. Spencer Bengal, your new helper."

"My new..." Missy was confused.

"Bengal, as in tiger?" Carla asked, peering over the top of her sunglasses for a better look.

"Yes, ma'am, like the tiger," he replied, with another killer grin.

"Rawr," Carla said, feeling mischievous.

"Down girl," Missy directed, shooting her a look. "Spencer, I didn't know that I had a helper," she said, wondering what on earth was going on.

"I was just hired today. Miss Maggie said that you needed a handyman, server, bartender, and helper at your tea room next door, so I guess I'm just supposed to go wherever I'm needed," he shrugged amiably.

"Oh, I hadn't realized that she'd begun taking applications yet," Missy blinked, absorbing the new information.

"I didn't fill out an application," Spencer said. "I just came by, had an interview, and she hired me on the spot."

"I bet she did," Carla leered playfully. Missy raised an eyebrow at her.

"Well, it was great meeting you two. I've gotta get back inside – I'm cleaning out the deep freeze. Have a great day," he waved cheerfully and headed back toward the Inn.

"Were you watching his behind as he walked away?" Carla drawled, after Spencer had gone inside.

"No! Of course not," Missy protested. "Shame on you, he's young enough to be your child!"

"Yes, he is," she grinned and pulled her sun hat down over her eyes once again.

Chapter 20

"So, now that you have a hunky helper, does that mean that you won't need my help any longer?" Echo asked, sounding rather forlorn.

"No, absolutely not!" Missy exclaimed. "Maggie has enough projects over at the inn to keep him busy for at least a year or so."

Her friend breathed a sigh of relief. "Okay, good, because I haven't quite made up my mind as to whether I'm going to stay here or go back to California."

"You know what my vote on that issue would be," Missy smiled fondly at her best friend.

"I know," Echo reached over and squeezed her hand. "That's the biggest part of wanting to stay," she admitted. "I miss you when I'm gone."

"Does a certain very talented artist have anything to do with your decision?" she asked with a sly smile.

"Kel is great...almost too good to be true it seems, but, given my track record when it comes to choosing men, I'm not going to allow the way that I feel about him to impact my decision one way or the other," she vowed.

"Well, you know that you can stay here as long as you'd like," Missy reminded her.

"I know. You and Chas are awesome, and I really

appreciate your hospitality. I want to figure out what I'm going to do so that I can either go back to California or find a place of my own here."

"Don't you have a house or something out there?"

"Nope, I rented after I left Louisiana, and when I decided to come surprise you, I ended my lease and put all of my stuff in storage," Echo explained.

"Wow. Well, you take your time, and when you get it figured out, you let me know."

"I will," she replied with a grateful smile. "Hey, Missy...?"

"Yes, darlin'?"

"I'm so glad I came out here," Echo confessed.

"Me too, honey. Me too."

This was an exciting book for me on so many levels. I had seventeen Cozy Mysteries under my belt at this point, nearly four years ago, and finally felt like I was sort of getting the hang of it. The characters had become old friends and there were some relational things going on that were starting to get pretty interesting. Conflict between rival friends, a touch of potential romance, and of course the adoration between Missy and Chas gave this book a truly sweet feel.

I did have one negative review on the book that made me laugh – I considered that progress – I laughed rather than cried. The person who didn't enjoy the book noted that some of the characters were 'just weird,' which I took as a compliment. To me, that meant that the characters were real. Real people have quirks and problems and interesting ways of dealing with everyday life, that's what makes life so wonderful and exciting. If we were all the same and always reacted in predictable ways, how awful would that be?

Probably the single most exciting thing about this book, however, was the introduction of Spencer. I had developed this character to be a focal and fascinating part of the rest of the series. He brings a mystery of his own, and will give incredible insight into Chas' background eventually as well. Spencer is a kind, helpful, all-around good guy, who becomes a key member of the Calgon family. He's also loosely modeled after one of my all-time favorite Marine veterans, my son.

This book is the beginning of a new era for Missy, Chas and the gang, and my hope was that it would entice the readers to ride out the rest of the series, which, even now, four years later, is still going. Thank you so much, dear readers, for traveling to Calgon with me one more time and hanging out with Missy and the gang. Stick around, we'll show you some good ole southern hospitality!

Pumpkin Spice Cupcakes

Cupcakes

1 15 oz can pumpkin puree

2 eggs

1 cup plus 2 Tbsp brown sugar

2 Tbsp unsalted butter at room temperature

2 tsp dried pie spice

½ tsp ground ginger

1 tsp pumpkin pie extract

3 Tbsp vanilla yogurt

½ cup milk

¼ cup vegetable oil

2 cups All-Purpose flour minus 2 Tbsp flour

2 Tbsp corn starch

1 tsp baking powder

1 tsp baking soda

Beat together pumpkin puree, eggs, butter, sugar, pie extract, yogurt, milk, and vegetable oil.

Sift together flour, baking powder, baking soda, pie spices, ginger, and corn starch.

Fold dry mixture into the wet ingredients.

Preheat oven to 350 degrees.

Pour batter to fill 2/3 of the cupcake liner.

Bake cupcakes for 15-17 minutes and check with a toothpick. If the batter does not stick to toothpick, then the cupcakes are done.

Makes 18-24 cupcakes.

Cream Cheese Frosting

8 oz cream cheese at room temperature

¼ cup unsalted butter at room temperature

2 cups powdered sugar

½ cup heavy whipping cream

1 tsp pure vanilla extract

2 Tbsp sour cream

Beat cream cheese and butter until fluffy.

Stir in sour cream and vanilla.

On low speed, alternating, blend in powdered sugar and heavy whipping cream until smooth and desired consistency.

Frost cupcakes when cooled.

Also by Summer Prescott

Frosted Love Series

Book 1: A Murder Moist Foul

Book 2: A Pinch of Murder

Book 3: Half Baked Murder

Book 4: A Mouthful of Murder

Book 5: Cupcakes and Murder

Book 6: Orange Marmalade Murder

Book 7: Buttercream Murder

Book 8: Teddy Bear Murder

Book 9: Honey Dripped Murder

Book 10: Devil's Food Murder

Book 11: Cereal Cupcake Murder

Book 12: Plain Vanilla Murder

Book 13: Strawberry Murder

Book 14: Raspberry Creme Murder

Book 15: Mango Madness Murder

Book 16: Chocolate Filled Murder

INNcredibly Sweet Series

Book 1: Irish Creme Killer

Book 2: Coconut Creme Killer

Book 3: Caramel Creme Killer

Book 4: Chai Cupcake Killer

Book 5: Streusel Creme Killer

Book 6: Peaches and Creme

Book 7: Marshmallow Creme Killer

Book 8: Boston Creme Killer

Book 9: Bourbon Creme Killer

Book 10: Spiced Latte Killer

Book 11: Toffee Apple Killer

Book 13: Peppermint Mocha Killer

Book 14: Sweetheart Killer

Book 15: Killer Me Green

Book 16: Blue Suede Killer

Cupcakes in Paradise Series

Author's Note

I'd love to hear your thoughts on my books, the storylines, and anything else that you'd like to comment on—reader feedback is very important to me. My contact information, along with some other helpful links, is listed below. If you'd like to be on my list of "folks to contact" with updates, release and sales notifications, etc.... just shoot me an email and let me know. Thanks for reading!

Also...

... if you're looking for more great reads, I am proud to announce that Summer Prescott Books publishes several popular series by Cozy authors Gretchen Allen and Patti Benning, as well as Carolyn Q. Hunter, Blair Merrin, Susie Gayle and more!

Contact Summer Prescott Books Publishing

Twitter: @summerprescott1

Blog and Book Catalog: http://summerprescottbooks.com

Email: summer.prescott.cozies@gmail.com

And...look up The Summer Prescott Fan Page and Summer Prescott Publishing Page on Facebook – let's be friends!

To download a free book, and sign up for our fun and exciting newsletter, which will give you opportunities to win prizes and swag, enter contests, and be the first to know about New Releases, click here: http://summerprescottbooks.com

Made in the USA
Middletown, DE
22 July 2019